This book belongs to:

_____

THE CLUB JEFFERY BOOK SERIES

READING BUDDIES DAY!

Andrew Critelli

Get The Free Awesome Affirmation Coloring Cards at:
www.ClubJeffery.com

Business Inquiries: info@andrewcritelli.com

Reading Buddies Day!
ISBN: 978-1-989822-00-5

Dedication:
To all the life-long readers.

It was another successful week. The only thing that stood between me and my weekend video game playing was our Friday afternoon Reading Buddies period.

Reading Buddies is where we have to read to the little kindergarten kids for a whole period. It was pretty genius on the part of our teachers. Because we have to do all the work, while they would get to chit chat and take a break from teaching and not have to do anything!

I hated it. Because it was just one giant hurdle that I had to overcome before I had my weekend freedom.

I was always paired up with the same partner.
A girl named Ganeet.

She was not really into variety. She always wanted
me to read her favorite book. It was some story about
a Snow Princess.

Ganeet was an excellent reader. She would also read
the story back to me over and over and over again.

I have heard the story sooooooo many times that I had
it memorized and didn't even need to look at the words
anymore.

Not only did Ganeet love the book, but after the book was read, she would want to talk about it and discuss every part in elaborate detail.

If I had to read the story one more time I feel like that would be the end of reading for me.

I believe that some books should have a legal limit to the amount of times that they can be read.

While walking to the Kindergarten room with my class one Friday, I made sure that I was in the back of the line. I wanted as little time in there reading as possible.

When I got inside I noticed everyone reading with their partners. I looked all over the room. But I didn't see Ganeet anywhere. She would always run up to meet me and annoyingly grab my hand to go sit on the carpet.

I asked where Ganeet was. Her teacher told me that she was away this week and that I could join a group to make a group of three.

Yesss!! I thought this was great! I tried not to look too excited and joined another group and hung out with them for the period. I didn't even have to do that much.

The following weeks felt strange. Ganeet wasn't at school for the next two weeks.

I later found out that Ganeet was sick and getting treatment at the hospital.

The school was even doing a fundraiser to help her and her family.

I went home that day and sat down in the kitchen. My Mom had just made a fresh batch chocolate chip cookies but I turned them down because I wasn't hungry.

She also asked if I was going to play my video games but I said I wasn't in the mood for that either.

My Mom then asked me what was wrong. She always knew when something was bothering me.

I explained what was going on. She told me to hold on a minute and made a few phone calls. It turns out that one of my Moms friends knows Ganeet's Mom.

We got in the car and left for the hospital. On our way to the hospital we made a couple of stops to grab a few things.

At the hospital I got to meet Ganeet's parents.

I introduced myself and told them that I was Ganeet's reading buddies partner. I also told them that I missed seeing her these past weeks as I shook their hands.

Ganeet's parents said that it was nice to meet me. And that Ganeet has talked a lot about me and that she really enjoys reading with me.

Then Ganeet's Mom told me that I could go in and see her.

I walked into the hospital room and saw Ganeet's eyes light up and she had a huge smile on her face.

I gave her a big giant hug and handed her the bag that we brought.

She loved the presents.

We brought a Super Teddy Bear and...

Our favourite book.

I asked Ganeet when she would be coming back to school.

She said it would be soon, probably next week.
I looked over at her parents and they smiled and nodded.

Ganeet then told me how much she loved school and that
she especially loves our Reading Buddies Day!

I told her... that I felt the same way too.

I can't wait for the next big day. :)

<u>Enjoy Reading Buddies Day even more!</u>
Draw the cover of your favorite book.

P.S.
How much fun is it to read?

See you next time for another big day!! :)

Up next... book #3
NINJA DAY!

See you there!! :)

Made in the USA
Columbia, SC
23 December 2022

74018775R00015